OTHER BOOKS BY HANS DE BEER

Little Polar Bear
Ahoy There, Little Polar Bear
Little Polar Bear Finds a Friend
Little Polar Bear, a Pop-Up Book
Little Polar Bear and the Brave Little Hare
Ollie the Elephant

BOOKS ILLUSTRATED BY HANS DE BEER

The Big Squirrel and the Little Rhinoceros by Mischa Damjan
Meet the Molesons by Burny Bos
Prince Valentino by Burny Bos

Copyright © 1994 by Nord-Süd Verlag AG, Gossau Zürich, Switzerland
First published in Switzerland under the title Kleiner Braunnär wovon träumst du?
English translation copyright © 1994 by North-South Books Inc.

First published in the United States, Great Britain, Canada,
Australia, and New Zealand in 1994 by North-South Books,
an imprint of Nord-Süd Verlag AG, Gossau Zürich, Switzerland.

Distributed in the United States by North-South Books Inc., New York.

Library of Congress Cataloging-in-Publication Data is available.
A CIP catalogue record for this book is available from The British Library.
ISBN 1-55858-294-0 (TRADE BINDING)
ISBN 1-55858-295-9 (LIBRARY BINDING)

1 3 5 7 9 TB 10 8 6 4 2
1 3 5 7 9 LB 10 8 6 4 2
Printed in Belgium

Bernard Bear's Amazing Adventure

WRITTEN AND ILLUSTRATED BY
Hans de Beer

Translated by Marianne Martens

North-South Books
NEW YORK / LONDON

Bernard Bear was sitting in front of his cave at the edge of the forest. It was a beautiful day, but even so, Bernard was feeling a little sad. While he was sitting there basking in the warm sunshine, a leaf had fallen off a tree and drifted down in front of him. Bernard was still a young bear, but he knew what this meant: Summer was over and winter would soon be on its way.

Bernard hated winter. When he was a baby bear, he would spend winters with his family in a big cozy cave. Those were nice winters. But last year Bernard had to spend his first winter alone, and after hibernating by himself, week after week, he had become very lonely.

Bernard thought that all the bears in the forest should spend their winters together in one big bear cave. He suggested this to the others, but when they heard his idea, they shook their heads. "You're just too lazy to build your own cave," one bear snapped.

"I hate cold weather," Bernard said sadly as he started to waterproof his cave.

"Why don't you head south like me?" suggested a little swallow. "Sunshine, palm trees, sand, and sea!" she twittered as she soared up in the air and disappeared.

"What a great idea!" Bernard said to himself.

He waited until all the other bears were in their caves for the winter, and set off. "Sunshine, palm trees, sand, and sea—*here I come!*" he shouted.

Bernard walked and walked and walked and walked, and by the next day he realized that he was hopelessly lost. The forest was cold and windy, and Bernard had no idea which way was south. Thinking about nice warm weather was the only thing that prevented him from turning around and going back to his lonely cave.

Soon it started to snow. The wind blew through Bernard's fur, and snow crystals burned his eyes. "How far south is the south?" Bernard muttered as he trudged along.

When it finally stopped snowing, Bernard was very tired and cold. He yawned and rubbed his eyes, and then stopped and stared. There, in the middle of the forest, was an old pick-up truck, covered with snow.

"If I can get the door open, I could climb in and warm up a bit," Bernard told himself. "I'll just catch forty winks and then be back on my way."

"I wonder what is in there," Bernard thought as he carefully wiped the snow off the window. He peered into the truck and saw three very surprised dormice looking back at him. Dormice sleep for seven long winter months, but these three had woken up when they heard Bernard. Frightened and wide awake, they began to scream: "Help! Help! A bearrrr!"

As politely as possible, Bernard asked the dormice if perhaps, under the circumstances—just for one night of course, certainly not any longer than that—could he perhaps come in and just rest a bit?

"No! Not now! Not ever!" shouted the most courageous dormouse.

"I'm sorry. At the moment we have no vacancy," continued the second dormouse.

"As you can see," squeaked the third, "this truck is completely full."

"And besides," said the first dormouse as he firmly locked the doors of the truck, "this is a nice clean truck! No place for a big wet brown bear like you."

Bernard was astonished.

"You won't let me in?" he growled. He was cold and tired, and he started to get a little angry with the dormice. After a while, he got VERY angry. He pushed the truck so that it rocked to and fro, and hammered at the doors with his paws. Then he jumped up and down on the roof until the dormice got seasick and finally had no choice but to let him in.

"Hello, I'm Bernard," he said, trying to be friendly. But the dormice didn't answer him. They just squeezed close to each other and glared at him.

Outside the snow started again and it got colder and colder. But in the truck, with Bernard's big body inside, it was warm and cozy. Before too long, everyone had fallen asleep, all curled up together. And slowly the truck once again became covered with snow.

Bernard woke with a big sneeze. He felt refreshed and happy, and rolled the side window down to take a look outside. Everything was covered with a blanket of snow, and there was a crystal clear winter sky over the forest. The three dormice were still sound asleep.

"Time to get to work," Bernard said softly as he climbed out of the truck.

Strange noises and fresh air soon awakened the dormice. They found Bernard happily banging around the engine. He told them about the swallow and about the sunshine, palm trees, sand, and sea.

"You think we'll make it with this old truck?" the smallest dormouse said fearfully, pointing to all the different engine parts lying around in the snow.

"But of course," yelled Bernard. "No problem at all."

"*No problem at all,*" squeaked the other two dormice.

After hours of work, some loud booms, and sputters and puffs of thick black smoke, the engine started to purr like a kitten. Bernard dug the truck out of the snow, everyone climbed inside, and they were on their way.

Before long, the snow was far behind them. And the farther they went, the louder the passengers sang. The dormice knew a lot of good songs, and Bernard Bear accompanied them with his deep bass voice. Bernard only rarely thought about his forest and the old family cave.

At one point Bernard stopped to ask a badger for directions. When Bernard told him where they were going, the badger said, "I've always wanted to go to the seaside. Would you mind if I joined you?"

"Of course not!" shouted the dormice. "We have plenty of room in the back of the truck."

As they drove along, they met many other animals who wanted to visit the beach, and soon the truck was full of all kinds of animals—singing loud, happy songs.

At last they reached the beach and parked the truck. They had made it! There was bright sunshine, palm trees, sand, and sea, just as the swallow had promised.

"Yippee!" shouted the animals as they ran to the water. Everyone talked about how wonderfully hot it was.

After a while Bernard and the dormice started to feel a bit *too* hot, so they went to lie down in the shade. But it was hot even in the shade, since they had thick winter coats.

'We didn't think it would be *this* warm," moaned the dormice.

"Me neither," wheezed Bernard. "It's terribly hot."

"Terribly, terribly hot," Bernard was murmuring to himself as he woke up. The sun shone onto his face. The three dormice were sleeping curled up on his chest. Bernard chuckled. "No wonder I was so hot!"

He yawned, and then jumped up out of the truck. The dormice tumbled off his chest and hopped out after him.

Bernard was standing outside looking around in surprise. "But . . . but . . . what about the palm trees?" he stammered. "I don't remember driving back from the sea."

"Sea? What are you talking about?" asked the dormice as they stretched in the warm spring sun. "We've been sleeping here for a long, long time!"

"What a wonderful dream you had!" said the dormice, when Bernard had finished telling them about the trip to the beach.

"You can certainly say that again," said Bernard.

But it had also been a wonderful hibernation—just like the old times, when Bernard spent the winter with his family in a big cozy cave. The dormice had slept completely undisturbed next to the big, warm, brown bear.

"We're sorry we tried to keep you out of the truck," said one of the dormice.

"We've never been so cozy and warm," said another with a sigh.

"Yes, it was cozy, wasn't it?" said Bernard.

Bernard started to think about his family and how much he missed them. He decided to go back home, but before he left, he made plans with the dormice for the next winter.

"Same time, same truck!" they called to each other. And just like real friends, the dormice waved to Bernard until they couldn't see him anymore.